Twelve Nights

Urs Faes

Twelve Nights

Translated from the German
by Jamie Lee Searle

Harvill *Secker*
LONDON

1 3 5 7 9 10 8 6 4 2

Harvill Secker, an imprint of Vintage, is part of the Penguin Random
House group of companies whose addresses can be found at
global.penguinrandomhouse.com

Penguin
Random House
UK

First published by Harvill Secker in 2020
First published with the title *Raunächte* in Germany by Insel Verlag in
2018

A CIP catalogue record for this book is available from the British Library

penguin.co.uk/vintage

ISBN 9781787301962

Published with the support of the Swiss Arts Council Pro Helvetia

Typeset in 13/18 pt Adobe Jenson Pro
by Integra Software Services Pvt. Ltd, Pondicherry

Printed and bound in Great Britain by Clays Ltd, Elcograf S.p.A.

Excerpt from 'Homecoming' by Paul Celan, translated by
Michael Hamburger, from *Poems of Paul Celan*, reprinted by kind
permission of Carcanet Press Ltd.

Penguin Random House is committed to a sustainable future for
our business, our readers and our planet. This book is made from
Forest Stewardship Council® certified paper.

For Silke Lucie

White, stacked into distance.
Above it, endless,
the sleigh track of the lost.

Below, hidden,
presses up
what so hurts the eyes,
hill upon hill,
invisible.

Paul Celan, 'Homecoming'

I

He placed one foot firmly in front of the other, as though each step had to leave an imprint in the snow. It was falling on this late afternoon too, whirling flakes in the grey that shrouded the town's porches and gables. He felt strangely unmoved as he passed them by, making his way along the road from the train station and towards the hill, unsettled that the streets were no longer the ones he had walked as a child. Only on the edge of town did he stop and look around, searching for traces of something familiar after his many years of absence.

His gaze was drawn into the grey mist, from which the tips of dark firs soared, their trunks veiled, making it look as though they were hanging, dangling, from invisible washing lines.

Only then did he hear the sound of trickling water and spot the parapet of the bridge, then the sign for the Schwarzer Adler inn and the yawningly empty space where the path branched off up the valley; a narrow, steep track along the stream, where willow trees sagged low to the ground beneath their burden of snow. Familiarity drifted towards him like an old melody, as though something that had been missing all these years had suddenly returned.

They used to walk this path every Sunday. He, his father, his mother and Sebastian, along with the others from the Schottenhöfe farms: the weekly church visit. He had paused for a while in the Zell parish church, Maria zu den Ketten, thinking about his mother, and Minna, who had loved its painting of the Virgin Mary. Whenever a day had become too much for her, Minna would set off with the words: 'I'm just walking to the church, it'll be like a little pilgrimage.' She would tell him the legends entwined with its history, including the one about Lene and Hans, the tragic lovers of the Black Forest. After all these years, he heard Minna's voice again; she was here. It was strange, yet undeniable.

The festive lights strung up in Zell's main street had reminded him that Christmas was approaching; there was shopping to be done.

He hadn't brought anything. His brother didn't care for presents. He flinched: if they would even see each other at all.

His hands clutched the straps of his rucksack; it was light, containing only a spare pair of gloves, two bread rolls and his water bottle. That was all he would need until he reached the inn, where his luggage awaited him; he had sent it ahead so he could make his way through the countryside on foot, an hour's walk perhaps, even if he took his time and stopped now and again to gaze at the valley's undulating landscape, its green-black pines huddled close and silent, making the day into night and the murmur of the treetops into an evensong. He wanted to make his way slowly: towards the houses, huts, stables and sheds that rose out of the snow-grey, to find his footing in this gradual process of familiarisation; a feeling of arrival that he hadn't felt in a long time – not since he had left.

He loved this land, even though after so many years it had become just a memory, and the autumn days in particular, when the harvest drew near and the orchard fruits, Boskoop and Jonagold apples, glistened, the vines on the hillsides full to bursting and the chestnuts' branches heavy with burrs; when the yellow potato leaves grew rampant across the furrows and the sun tumbled through the crowns of the ever more sparsely-leaved trees, becoming entangled in the foliage, making the dust grains dance, haloing the thinning larches and oaks of the forest. And he, out with his brother, Sebastian, long before their feud.

Back then, when the fields were fallow and sallow, the beech leaves deep brown and the weeping willows fused into a sombre copse, they had stood together, listening down into the ravine that yawned out from the Grafenberg, to the ravens cawing into the silence.

For a moment, he hoped that, by returning, he would be able to reconcile with this at once lost yet intimate landscape. Perhaps even find his way home? The names alone evoked closeness, the peak of the Kuhhornkopf jutting out of the walls of grey mist, the Hasenberg, the track through Hullert up to the Vogt auf Mühlstein inn; its name, too, containing secrets of times gone by.

He and Sebastian had often sat there with their father, wide-legged on the bench. In a silent harmony that had never even given rise to the thought that they might one day argue, much less over Minna.

He paused and listened, watching the mist sweep through the boughs of the trees and along the stream down the valley. They had built dams in the water, lowered their boats and let them drift, accompanied by midges buzzing around their heads and dragonflies darting to and fro across the riverbank.

Was he searching for something that had become lost over the years? The notion of something that was no longer there, that memory couldn't fill: something that had been buried, paralysed by shock, by rage?

They had often lost their way in these bushes that lined the water's edge, in these childhood hunting grounds which were theirs alone: he and Sebastian, out in the forest, with a wooden axe and bow and arrow, hunting buffalo and tracking bears, scrapping and scuffling with each other sometimes, but through it all devoted brothers who loved one another. Until the day when everything changed.

The Hinterhambach wine tavern appeared momentarily as the fog opened up and became mist thin, drawing the eye to the embankment, as though a curtain had lifted from the edge of the forest and down the hill to Hullert; to the small yard in front of his childhood home: that was where it had lain, the dying animal.

He shivered. The horrific deed caught up with him as though it had been yesterday and not forty years ago, as though everything was returning, even their footsteps from back then: an early photo of two young lads, like twins, cheek to cheek in a close embrace, their eyes shining brightly; one of them smiling at the other; a laugh, bold and brash.

Once again he came to a standstill. Everything was silent. Even the murmur of the stream seemed to be part of the silence, one which struck him, the city dweller he had become, not only as unfamiliar, but as unnatural. And within it the rushing sound of the fir trees from Reutegut and – here and there – the eerie call of the nocturnal birds.

And the humming? Would he hear it again? It was at this time in particular, as the year drew to a close, that they used to hear it around the house and farm; a faint whistling at the windows; a sudden draught of air; a stirring in the undergrowth and someone's shocked cry as they were pulled in. His mother had always heard it, fearing it, as Christmas approached. They start with the humming, she said, these nights, which she called the bleak nights. That was when she put the wind chimes on the balcony, along with a sprig of mistletoe and a linen sachet stuffed with Alpine leek and dried St John's wort. He had always loved the smell as she burned the herbs and let the smoke drift through the house: slightly sweet, spicily pungent, a hint of thyme, of heather and valerian, aromas of apple blossom and resin.

The image of his mother's face had always been there, all this time. Year in and year out, she had told stories about these nights, the Twelve Nights, Dodecameron, which threatened disorder and peril through the work of dark forces, the abysses gaping open: a disaster which drew ever closer, towards the feast of St Thomas, New Year's Eve, and Epiphany. She would put juniper berries in the incense burner, adding fir and spruce needles, an activity that seemed to calm her, as though it gave her stability and certainty. No misfortune could strike her then, neither her nor her family.

The ill fate their mother had feared, and hoped to prevent with all her precautions, did occur. But it wasn't the work of demons. They had conjured it up, he and Sebastian: the fraternal feud in Hullert. Or had it even been a war? No wind chime could prevent it, no sprig of mistletoe, no St John's wort; motherwort and sweet seneca were powerless, as was the Yule log smouldering in the yard.

He lifted his head and listened. Not a sound. The light snow fell silently. No humming, no owls hooting in the ravine, no scraping or screeching.

Back then, too, on that Saturday shortly after New Year when he had left the valley for ever, there had been nothing but silence; dark flocks of migrating birds had circled silently, black crows, here and there a blackbird, a tit. Then, once he was trudging towards the town, a piercing cry had sliced through the air.

He had taken it with him on his long journey across the ocean, together with that last glimpse of the Hullert ridge, with its tall fir, and the scent of snow and longing that lay over the valley.

Would the fir tree still be standing after all these decades? And the old well by the entrance to the house, with the thin rivulet of water that trickled out of the leaky pipe, the rust eating its way backwards from the spout?

Did he belong there?

Where did he belong? Where might he have belonged? On the farm; to Minna?

A return to a distant world, into the tracks of his childhood and his beginnings?

Would his brother come? Would they find their way back to words once more, beyond the hatred which ran like a dark spoor through the passing years, through a whole lifetime?

II

He closed the door behind him, stowed the key in his trouser pocket, paused in the corridor. He checked his coat. Did he have everything? Pen and notepad? Wallet? And the bag for his brother?

Outside, through the window, the snow was falling once more, in dense flakes on this early evening; a creeping dusk blurred the contours, turning the trees into wizened forms, the stream to a taffeta-grey ribbon, the farmhouses to shadowy distorting mirrors. The street could no longer be seen in the leaden gloom, which was tinged blue towards the forest, black down into the ravine. Childhoodland, filled with scents and stories, legends like that of the forest spirit Holländer Michel, figures looming out of the darkness of the trees, the meadows and marshlands, shallow waters and moon-pale quarry ponds.

The farm down below was a dim fleck, disintegrating. But into this shimmering, images settled: the foliage of a spring day, the wisteria leading to the garden; his mother in a headscarf, raking the vegetable plots; he and Sebastian on the bench, throwing their marbles. Vesper bells from the pilgrimage church echoed up through the valley, and someone came walking down the path, finding sanctuary in the candlelit chapel, a pilgrim seeking quiet reflection.

In the corridor, the dark wood panelling gleamed. He trudged slowly towards the window, almost colliding with one of the deer antlers that protruded from the walls. Timidly, he turned towards it, and was startled by the sight of the veiled eyes, staring threateningly at him from the white of the bones; he jumped aside.

At the window, he leaned his forehead against the glass. The stream glistened between the willow trees, flowing away in a winding course. He had often sat there with Sebastian when they climbed up to the hunters' lookout.

And down below, the Hullert farm, the family property, his former home, stretched its pointed roof up to the fir trees.

He heard voices coming from the bar, the clink of glasses, the scrape of chairs being pulled across the floor: it was suppertime. The landlord was serving. Speck and kirschwasser for those who wanted a little schnapps; blood sausage or pickled ham hock with farmhouse bread for those with empty, rumbling stomachs; or the warming soup with dumplings. The landlord was proud of his menu; that was why it had remained practically unchanged for decades. Even someone who had returned from the grave could have ordered from memory.

There were rarely guests from further afield at this time of year, the landlord had told him regretfully, but he stayed open for the locals, who liked to gather during these days, especially those who lived on the farms in pairs, or even alone, like Sebastian. There were more than a few like that. As Christmas approached, they came in more frequently for a drink or some supper, although Sebastian visited rarely or not at all. But perhaps he would this year, the landlord had added; the countryside wasn't the only thing made lonely by the snow.

He was still standing at the top of the stairs. He gave the deer antlers a nod, feeling more familiar with them already, and noticed a blueish film of dust on the edge of the bones. He blew on it, coughed, then stared back out into the snow, which was enveloping everything that had once had shape and colour.

He heard kitchen noises, a sizzling followed by a barrage of aromas: lard, onions, vegetable broth. Then shuffling footsteps, the creak of the wooden floor.

Everything all right?

The landlord looked up at him questioningly. He lifted his palm in greeting and slowly made his way downstairs, towards the open mouths. He shook the outstretched hands, listened to the names, sat down at the table, joined in a toast to the day and the year that was drawing to a close, to everything that lay behind them.

So you're the brother, then, of Sebastian in Hullert?

That's right. I'm Manfred.

You've been gone a long time.

He nodded.

Overseas.

The heavy-boned man, who introduced himself as Lutz, wore a cardigan made from coarse wool, somewhat baggy and felted, reinforced with leather patches at the elbows. He studied Manfred with a gaze which was at once shadowy and penetrating.

So, Sebastian's brother.

He took a swig of his drink.

It's cold out there. Could get icier still, and there's more snow to come. These are the bleak nights, after all.

Everyone stared out of the window into the white gloom.

The kobolds are shaking out their flour sacks.

Lutz laughed gruffly.

So you want to see your brother?

Manfred nodded again.

Lives alone, seldom shows his face. He's afraid of the Harmersbach valley folk. Afraid of everyone.

We're afraid too.

The landlord's interjection was a touch too loud, as though he were hurrying to drown out the sense of unease. These are fearful times in the world, he continued, nothing but disaster, war and massacre. The evil spirits are everywhere, even if you don't believe in them. And now, with a severe winter setting in, you can't even retreat into the woods. He took a deep swig of his beer.

It's no wonder the ghosts are stirring in the ravine, Lutz exclaimed. The dead are on the move again. You can hear the creaking, he said, pointing his finger up to the ceiling. Like in the old days.

Come on, there's no creaking. The landlord seemed irritated. Winter just puts you in a sour mood because you can't go off into your woods.

It's during these Twelve Nights that they wreak their havoc, Lutz declared stubbornly, everyone knows that. They're up there on the millstone, making it grind and grate. Don't you all hear it, out there, the moaning? They've come to haunt us.

But there was no moaning to be heard, only the sound of a door being slammed and the stamping of feet.

Evening all.

The newcomer nodded to the group and brushed the snow out of his thinning hair.

Evening, verger, they mumbled in chorus.

Landlord, it's high time you slit that sow's throat and brought it to the table for us to feast on. Lutz laughed once again, a rasping sound.

Drop it, Lutz. It's all nonsense.

That's what his father used to say, too, when at the winter solstice his mother strung up her sachets on the balcony, filled with tender concern for house and farm, for man and beast. This was always her way; she had once lured a wasp out of the bathroom with honey to avoid harming it, and carried a blindworm from the edge of the path into the protection of the grass.

He looked around at the group of men. Through their hearty gulps and deep glass-gazing, they were becoming increasingly animated and loud.

It's the women's time, grunted Lutz. Holda and Perchta are making a racket already.

What nonsense; there are no hordes of women, no hosts of spirits – just snow, and soon a new year!

The landlord was growing more impatient.

All that remains for us men is to drink ourselves silly. Cheers!

You always drink yourself silly.

Another Pilsner, landlord.

His mother's petite form darted through the room with the pan, its dried berries and grasses glinting festively. This had been a custom in her family, in the upper Rench valley, and one she had never let herself be dissuaded from, not even by his father's mockery. As she worked, she would tell them stories about the ghost of an old monk, with a pointed beard and buckled shoes, who wandered the valley's forested massif, and of the water spirits in the Mummelsee, which rose out of the depths when startled by a stone.

Manfred had often followed his mother around, in awe of the solemnity and devotion of her rituals. She wouldn't be swayed by anyone, not even the pastor, for whom this was a step too far, the burning of herbal concoctions to fumigate the house, again and again up to Epiphany, and the garden too, where she kindled fire even amidst deep snow.

She began gathering the plants in summer, by the stream, in the meadows, in the forest, labelling and drying them: juniper, St John's wort, oregano and toadflax. There was a carefulness to this, a love for all creatures, that he greatly admired. Ancestry, this was the word that came to mind, maintaining a connection with one's forefathers, the grandparents and parents; preserving a part of their lives, and, in doing so, a part of oneself.

She moved through the house and farm as her ancestors had, tending to her garden, her wisteria, her camellia, with almost exaggerated care, as though they were breathing creatures. Perhaps, although she herself wouldn't have described it as such, there was a kind of reverence to this, a silent gratitude for everything she had learned from them, everything they had given her.

Sebastian was very similar to their mother; perhaps it had been she who wanted him to inherit the farm, even though he had so often acted clumsily, awkwardly, irritating their father.

Those hopeless amateurs, what a disaster! And we just bow our heads instead of rising up and marching, like in the old days, in the Peasants' War.

Lutz balled his fist. How long will it go on, that we just nod and put up with it? Are we our own cattle? A disaster, he repeated, drinking quickly and heavily; he spluttered and choked, his face turned red.

Everyone was silent.

Manfred closed his eyes.

His brother was alone, and almost snowed in. Should he go to him, knock on the door, instead of waiting here? Or send word, call him out into this bleak, snowy night, St Thomas' Night? To talk about the ghosts of the forest and the past that sometimes roamed through his dreams, especially since the illness, as though something unresolved were returning, knocking on the farmhouse door, demanding admission and presence. So much in his life had remained unresolved. These were the ghosts which filled his Twelve Nights. The ones from folklore, he didn't believe in, but he did believe in his own; they too were nocturnal hordes, as terrifying as the processions of the dead out in the fields. And Minna? Was she one of them? She was always there. Encased within the cocoon of images, in the love that never faded, not even after years and decades had passed.

He wouldn't go to her grave.

Lutz banged his glass down on the table.

Don't you want to hear it, landlord? It's creaking because the world is out of joint; the dead are on the move; the old spirits are stirring.

That's nonsense, the dead aren't going anywhere, not in this weather. What shivering, frozen souls they would be. It's a harsh winter, it's snowing – and on your soul too, Lutz. The landlord clapped him on the shoulder.

Mock me all you like, but the old monk will hunt you down and curse you with the lumbago, or set an epidemic among your livestock.

Tell him to send us the water nymph from Waldsee instead, we'd give her a warm welcome.

The desultory comment came from the verger.

These are the nights of portent, said Lutz, when the die is cast on fortune or ruin. Yours too, landlord. The ghosts are moaning out there, you can hear them loud and clear, especially over with Sebastian on the Hullert farm.

With Sebastian?

Manfred looked up at Lutz questioningly.

The landlord hesitated, then spoke up. He's become a little eccentric. Too much bad luck.

Bad luck, is that what you'd call it? Lutz's voice turned scornful.

Come with me. The landlord nodded towards the dining room. It's quieter back there.

Manfred followed him. Bettine brought their glasses, then pulled the door shut as she left.

Zum Wohl, said the landlord, raising his glass. He hesitated for a moment, then continued to speak. They've fallen out, he said, some dispute over a sick cow. Ever since, Lutz has been blaming Sebastian, unjustly, for everything that goes wrong in the valley.

What's going on with Sebastian?

The landlord sighed.

A long run of bad luck that started almost as soon as your parents passed. First the epidemic among his livestock, then the business with Minna. She went into a home, stopped talking, and a short while later … well, you know the rest. Now she's buried out there. It was all too much. It would be too much even for the likes of us.

He paused.

The business with Minna, especially, was more than someone like him could take. She was a good wife to him, always stood by him, not just in the farm work and at home, but in all his worries, in everything that went wrong. A wife, and a friend. And then she was gone. Fallen into silence, into speechlessness. She went into the home, then beneath the earth. So unexpected. And then on top of all that came the conflict with Lutz. Conflict with everyone. Sebastian was even out of harmony with the farm, the weather, the animals.

And no one left there but him.

Not even a child or grandchild to visit him. Friends? Does a man like him have friends? A man who doesn't go to the inn, who won't show his face at gatherings, not even the parish fair. It's no wonder someone like that becomes ill, frail. The bones can no longer carry the misery. The pain hits the small of the back first, then the hips, the knees. And the person begins to limp, as if it weren't enough already, with a shuffling gait, dragging steps.

And why?

The curse, he always said. His brother's curse.

What?

The landlord avoided his gaze and swallowed heavily.

You cursed your brother. In anger.

It was just one of those things said in the heat of the moment. Out of hurt. That's all.

Everyone gets angry sometimes. Surely no one believes in a curse?

Sebastian does.

The landlord's tone was light but firm.

It defies belief, so much misfortune. One blow after another. But more about that later. Perhaps he'll come by and tell you himself.

Does he sometimes, then?

He looked at the landlord inquisitively.

Does he sometimes come up to the inn and sit with the other men? And what does he talk about, what does he say of the farm, the animals, himself?

The landlord hesitated.

He says little, very little. He barely talks, he's the silent type. Hardly eats. A bowl of soup at most. And he doesn't drink much either. Only in moderation. He's moderate in everything. Sometimes you want to give him a good shake, to shake the composure – or maybe it's lethargy – right out of him. Perhaps that's what irritates Lutz, this obstinate calm. As though nothing can unsettle him. But what happened with Minna, that must have affected him.

The landlord fell silent for a moment.

What was he like before? Did he talk much as a child? And later?

Manfred looked up.

He was a quiet child, certainly, but he spoke, at home around the table. Maybe he wasn't brimming over with words, but still. Different. That's what my mother once said; Sebastian is different.

He broke off.

What did he really know about his brother? How had he been with Minna? What had they talked about? Had theirs been a wordless love? One that didn't need any words? Secure within something that went beyond speech?

Were Minna and Sebastian really in love?

The landlord looked up, seemingly at a loss.

No one knows. They never came to the inn together. You would see them working alongside each other in the fields, harvesting potatoes and turnips, felling trees. And they came to the parish fair from time to time. But other than that?

All of a sudden, he stood up.

Work's calling.

They stepped out into the corridor. The landlord headed off towards the kitchen. Manfred watched him go, then pushed open the door to the bar, slipping back into the dense smoke, waving his hand through the fug.

There they sat at the broad wooden table: Lutz, talking more than anyone else; Bunzenbach, from Schnaitberg – a farm near Nordrach amongst a sparse scattering of pines, the landlord had explained; and the verger from the pilgrimage church was still there too, a stern, pastoral figure in his shirt, clerical collar and waistcoat.

The landlady was serving the food: plates of scrambled eggs, potato soup steaming in its pot, cheese and sausage on the side.

Sit down and join us, there's plenty of room.

The Schnaitberg farmer's voice was slightly croaky; his arm, waving vigorously, resembled a rudder.

Manfred sat down.

Lutz was in the midst of an angry tirade about the price of milk. It was still below cost, the farmers were making losses.

We've nothing left to live on, and now the wood's getting scarce too. It's hopeless.

Manfred winced.

Zum Wohl.

The verger raised his glass.

Let's stay positive, it can't hurt. *Zum Wohl.*

Noting the heaviness in his limbs, Manfred stood up.

It's time for me to turn in, gentlemen. Good evening to you.

He left the table, slowly climbed the stairs and stepped into his room. Opening the window, he brushed the snow, the flakes downy and light, from the pane and the sill.

On the white hillside opposite, the contours of the Hullert farm were blurred; deep snow lay in the yard, on the roof, on the shrubs. No path had been cleared, not even from the road to the house, nor up the stone steps to the front door. A remembered image showed them on these steps: their shadows fell across the gravel, close together, one of them six years old, the other eight, in short trousers with turn-ups above the knees, both with thin legs and lanky torsos. Their stoutly built father wasn't in the picture, nor their mother. Just the two of them. Although Sebastian wasn't laughing, his expression seemed contented, carefree. He was holding in his hand something they had called a club, a misshapen, intergrown branch fork, an oval, its bark flaking. Their shoulders were touching. Sebastian was wearing his sand-coloured peaked cap, its band pulled down over his ears; he used to wear it all the time, even long after he started school. It had still hung in his room years later, faded and threadbare. The cap low over his forehead, his eyes shaded; his gaze was always like this, half-concealed.

The farm now lay in darkness; no light burned in any of the windows. Even the fir tree in front of the house was weighed down with snow, on every branch a seam of white: unsullied, unmarked, exposed. He recalled the two of them during one of these icy winters, outside in the cold, wrapped up yet still freezing; an endurance test on the bench, the sun a cold glimmer over the forest, whose trees were frozen over, a glass geometry. Sebastian was the one fascinated by the wintry bleakness of a world paralysed by ice, where even the birds could no longer be heard, not even owl calls; only frost-silence.

Did Sebastian still enjoy the winter now, the pure white in the valley and around the houses, the snow-covered pathways, the inertia?

Thin smoke billowed out of the chimney, a swift, swirling plume; it was immediately captured by a gust of wind, swept away, dispersed; then the smoke rose steadily again, uphill, grey on grey, a subtle quiver in the frigid air of the winter's night.

Would his brother come?

Would he sit down at the table, with that restrained momentum so characteristic for him, his movements clumsy, ungainly? Would he then, after a pause, begin to speak in his hesitant way? Or would they sit in silence, their hands laid on the table, the hands they'd used to grab each other as scrapping boys, rivals in a cockfight, boisterous but harmless.

Only years later, once they were adults, had they laid into each other for real, striking and hitting, incensed and unrelenting; enemies who despised each other.

Could it all have been prevented?

III

The next day, he saw immediately that there was no message in the letter rack. The landlord confirmed it, adding unasked that there had been no light at his brother's farm the entire night, nor had the snow been cleared from the entrance; and there were no footprints.

What does that mean?

His voice betrayed his anxiety.

The landlord looked around him.

It's often like that. Silent around the house, the shutters closed, no movement, no one to be seen or heard. Only the smoke from the chimney to show there's someone in there, moving from room to room, perhaps fishing the post out of the letter box from time to time. If any post ever comes, that is.

How can a person live like that, alone with only the animals? Wouldn't they eventually turn to stone? First their heart, then their body?

The landlord shrugged.

Since Minna's been gone, it seems abandoned. Vacant.

Manfred flinched, and couldn't bring himself to look at the landlord. What had happened within Minna, to disturb her, push her into silence?

Vacant?

That was how the farm had seemed to him all those years ago, when he had walked away from it before dawn: a cold, damp morning, the end of the Holy Night on which fortune had favoured his brother and not him. The first light after that night of snowfall was bleak and faint; the sun a pallid, glimmering disc in the grey sky. The call of owls came from the pine forest like a wail, a scream from the depths.

Then the humming, which got louder and louder. For the first time ever, he found himself believing in the evil spirits, in the demon army of kobolds that had taken possession of the house. In defiance of the wind chimes and herb sachets on the balcony, in defiance of the smouldering Yule log and juniper, they had forced their way into the hearts of its inhabitants, his father's, his mother's, his brother's. And what about Minna? Would she side with them too? Since time immemorial, marriages in the valley had taken place according to land, not love. That was the rule and always had been. Even if it was no longer spoken, the roots ran deep. On that Christmas morning, he had still hoped that Minna would stay and walk life's path with him, not in Hullert, but somewhere else – in Mergelfeld or Mittelbach, or even their beloved Rheinauen, where an uncle of Minna's had horses and tobacco fields. They had sometimes gone riding there, through sedge meadows, reed beds and marshy lowlands, past white and pollarded willows, feeling like they were in the prairies, or the Amazon rainforest. He and Minna, defiant in their love, just like Lene and Hans. They had so many plans back then, not just for the Hullert farm, but for horse-breeding in the Black Forest, or even a farm overseas, in Canada perhaps. They had once searched for land in Kinzigtal, visiting villages, farmsteads, riding out into the landscape. On that Christmas morning, he had still believed in their plans, in their love.

He had heard the bells from the pilgrimage church, which rang out during Advent for the Rorate Mass, for the dawn of the light. The bells were often accompanied by other figures from the farms, wrapped up warmly against the cold, who were drawn through the snow and storm long before breakfast to the church, which was illuminated only by candles, a sea of light in which they paused for a while, amid the descending silence.

He had looked up at the house for a moment; there was nothing to be seen, nothing to be heard. They're sleeping in blissful peace, he had thought to himself bitterly; only he was still in turmoil, incensed by what had happened. So out of the blue that he hadn't wanted to believe or acknowledge it. The conspiracy. The betrayal. All of a sudden, the poison of blind hatred had surged within him. The lot had fallen in favour of his brother, not him.

Perhaps he could have predicted it even before the Christmas festivities began. If he had only paid attention. Then he wouldn't have been taken unawares, and could have reacted

35

more calmly, and the situation wouldn't have spiralled out of control.

Where did Minna stand?

That was the question he asked himself that morning. All his hope was pinned on her.

Could he have read the signs, a turning away from him and towards his brother? *I'm fond of you both, but you're my great love*, she had said. And then she had looked at him, with that expression so completely without distrust. All his love belonged to Minna, unconditionally. It had done all these years.

To him, she was everything life had to give.

Minna had opened up new paths for him. He never forgot that. Paths out into the countryside, from the Vogt's house and across to the clearing atop the densely wooded Flacken hills, then down along the banks of the Regelsbach, to Schrofen, or along the Rühlsbach into the Stollengrund glade. It was she who had taught him to listen: to the susurration of the winter twilight below the Mooskopf; to the cry of a bird at the Haldeneck viewpoint; to the roaring of the fallow deer in the ravine. Minna knew paths through both wood and meadow, and took him along on horseback or simply on foot, up the valley to Heidenkirche, where moss and ferns grew across the sandstone rock formations, speckled with grass, where dark chambers and crevices opened up, beckoning into the underworld: at one time, distant gods were worshipped in these caves. Or she led him to the monastery ruins up on Allerheiligenberg, so isolated they seemed beyond this world. And just the two of them there. They had so often sought out remote places, especially when they were going through a difficult time, struggling with the world and with love, out of harmony with themselves, with the lives they were living. So many plans and so few days lived, their gazes trained on the future, the present still slight.

They had wanted to marry in a place like that, he and Minna. In accordance with the age-old wording that holds two people together for ever. With Minna, it would have been for ever. And for eternity. His words were so elaborate when he thought of her back then. And they had never stopped being so.

*

Why could he still not be here without being reminded of her? Why was every step he took into this landscape a step towards her, even now, after decades had passed? And one still accompanied by pain? Was this what had brought him back to the valley of his childhood?

She had walked beside him quietly and unobtrusively, wearing her sturdy shoes, blue jacket, and the rucksack from which she would occasionally pass him something: an apple, a piece of bread, the water bottle; an attentiveness which was instinctive.

Minna was there, always completely herself: the kind of person you want to take in your arms.

He wondered about the origins of this strange tenderness he felt towards her, which had never faded, not even long after she became Sebastian's. As though some part of him were still with her. It flickered again and again, even far away in his overseas exile, and had awakened once more as he made his way from the train station into the Harmersbach valley: to the Vogt auf Mühlstein, to the Grafenberg, to

Reutegut and up to the Taschenkopf. These places remained intertwined with Minna, with the sound of her voice recounting Lene and Hans' sad fate. She knew the paths they had taken and the places they had lingered in, including right here, by this crucifix. Lene had stood on this very spot, pleading, imploring, for happiness in love.

He pictured the two of them before him, as though centuries hadn't passed and their tale was no longer history, but taking place here and now. It was Minna's story, told to him on an early evening beneath a vast accumulation of cloud in the Nordrach valley, amid the dusty odour of the chalky paths on the Stollenberg. He listened as Minna spun the threads of her narrative, following the lovers' footsteps, their furtive embraces. He felt her hand in his, and within it, everything he felt for her.

Minna's almost reverent pace, which seemed to invite one to pause, was notched with images, colours, with the vibrant orange of the pumpkins in the brackish water of the swampy hollows, where the sounds became trapped – the chirr of a robin, the dull whirr of the telegraph poles.

Minna remained. She was there in her gestures, a passed apple or mug of tea or one of the biscuits made from flour and sugar, and also in the little gifts she gave from time to time; she would place something down casually, a small package, a flower, a stone with unusual veining. It was always something oddly characteristic of Minna, selected with care, lovingly wrapped or arranged, striking and priceless for that reason alone and expressing a great deal about the person who had found, crafted and gifted it. That was Minna. The seahorse had always remained close to his person; the shell with sand from the ocean had survived every move.

Had he idealised her, and failed to read signs of disharmony between them?

Would Sebastian still come? Or send word?

The landlord looked at him quizzically, then shrugged twice in quick succession.

We're setting the dining room for two, a celebratory meal: soup with dumplings, then roasted pork shoulder with mash and cabbage, and rye bread. My wife has already made a start on the baking.

The landlord beamed.

Manfred smiled back.

I'll just walk up the valley a little, along the stream and through the pines to the Vogt auf Mühlstein.

You won't find any bride waiting there, the landlord observed.

Then down Hutmacherdobel to Mühlen-stüble.

Wrap up warm, the wind's howling over the summit and down through the whole valley. His tone turned serious. Many a person has misjudged the storms and fallen in the snow, stumbled into the brook or the ravine, or frozen to death and been carted straight off to the morgue. Winter claims one or two victims every year here in the valley. That's how the Vogt, Anton Muser, met his sad end back then. Winter returned with full force as late as March, and he fell and froze to death not far from the Stollengrund clearing. No one heard his cries, yet he must have been there for hours.

A terrible way to die.

The landlord made a tutting sound.

His was a terrible way to live, too. It was a crime against love he committed, standing in its way to marry off his daughter to that rich farmer. And then Lene faded away, and was lost.

That was all a long time ago. I'll be careful, Manfred reassured the landlord. I may have been gone a long time, but I'm no stranger to these parts. I know the paths and forests, and the ravines too.

He took the same path as he had taken back then, also on Christmas Day, after the shocking revelation. He had tramped through the dense, driving snow, up past the hunter's lookout to the rocky ledge on the far side of the valley, and sat down on a tree stump above Michaelsfelsen. The snowflakes that fell onto his cap and into his face had done nothing to cool his rage; his balled fists had pounded against a tree trunk.

Amongst the dark, grey-veiled trees, all he could ever see was his family standing there; his father festive in his Sunday best, his cufflinks gleaming, his arm circling their mother's hips. Her hand rested on his brother's belt, the three of them one conspiratorial entity. In that moment, he had spotted around his mother's neck the little linen sachet, containing the tiny bones whose residual energy was said to ward off evil spirits.

He had only been gone for three weeks, on a trip to Styria.

What had happened in his absence? What had forged them together?

His father's words were uttered almost casually, his larynx barely hopped. He looked past him as he spoke: about the farm, which, well, would be going to his brother –

His mother lowered her gaze, her hand trembled slightly, he saw it as she grasped his father's arm. His brother stood unmoving, his eyes suppressing the triumph, as though he had rehearsed it.

But that wasn't supposed to –

Manfred's protest exploded out of him like a scream –

– No, that wasn't the original plan, but it's better this way, Sebastian will take on the farm.

His father's interjection was swift, with a glance at his wife, at Sebastian, who both nodded in agreement, looking at one another. The father reached for the bottle, which had already been opened, the mother handed him the glasses.

It was all prepared, thought Manfred, orchestrated.

His father poured; the gurgling sound tumbling into the inert silence that was expanding through the room, stretching, bending.

Even as his father grasped the glass, Manfred staggered out. He had to get away. To Minna's. No. Minna wasn't there, and wouldn't be back until New Year, if at all, for perhaps she was already part of it, in agreement even, loving his brother more than him after all. This fear had never faded, and could cut through even the most tender moments with her: an abyss opening up in the day. And yet she never let any doubt arise about whom she cared for as a friend and whom she really loved. Even a high-spirited gesture towards his brother never carried ambiguity. So why was he left with this fear? Was it a premonition, which came true on this Christmas Day?

Now he tramped once more through the deep snow, following the flight of the crows, hearing the bells from the pilgrimage church; a mellow sound that drifted through the cold air and fell into his ears. He had met Minna by the church countless times, she had told him how an image of the Virgin Mary was found in a nearby rose-bush, and how the locals named it Mary of the Rose and built the chapel. Many years ago, another lover, Magdalene – Lene – had also spent time there, lamenting her sorrow.

Every time he made his way up the valley and neared the Vogt's former residence, he pictured them before him: Lene and Hans, the lovers who were kept apart by the girl's merciless father, who had opposed their union and forced her into marriage with the rich farmer. On these paths he had so often walked, the lovers had found hidden spots where they could steal brief moments together, like the narrow track between Mühlstein and Stollengrund that led into the gloomy undergrowth of the forest, where no one would see them. Or along the slippery uphill path which Lene had often taken after dusk, making her way towards Hans, humming softly in the semi-darkness to banish her fear, to drown out the noises which drifted over from the Grafenberg and up from the stream; a nocturnal rasping or rattling, a whimpering or groaning, and sometimes, comfortingly, blackbird song, the hammering of a woodpecker, the cuckoo's cleft call.

Singing helped on occasion, as did the knowledge that Hans was getting closer, making his way from the neighbouring valley where he had a straw mattress in his humble dwelling in the mill loft, up the Stollenberg, towards her, to Lene.

Recounting the tale, Minna had the lovers walk through the pine thicket, trek along rain-soaked paths, among stinging nettles and tall ferns, out into clearings where wild flowers bloomed, larkspur and mullein, fire lilies and February daphne. These places were remote, secluded, where no one would disturb their lovers' games. Walking and narrating, she created the same secret trysts for herself and Manfred; winding paths and enchanted spots, as though only a love told were a real love.

Hans and Lene had often stood in the sunken lane, on the small incline where they met for the last time. They held one another tightly, as though they were sinking into the ground. This was the very spot where, years later, the hard-hearted Vogt had stumbled in the snow, where his cries went unheard and he froze to death; the late winter as ruthless to him as he had been towards the lovers.

Minna's voice carried a hint of satisfaction as she spoke those words.

For him and Minna, there had been no last meeting. No wayside shrine served as a reminder of their love. Only inside him, spun within a deep cocoon, did their love live on.

A cold wind rippled the snow; white flames licking across the slope. He followed the clearing uphill, towards Sodlach. That was where he had discovered the hunters' tree stand; the rungs of the ladder lined with frozen domes of snow. He and his brother, in high spirits, had climbed up it and jumped down again and again, each time venturing a step higher, the tingling in their bellies stronger, their hesitation greater, again and again until Sebastian had fallen and broken his leg. Manfred had carried his younger brother slowly back down the valley, the two of them united by their close bond.

And after this Christmas and its revelation, what now? He had screamed his question out into the winter's day, which swallowed his voice and made the farms appear small, unremarkable.

He strode onwards just as he had back then, as though decades hadn't passed since.

Minna hadn't only told him the story, she had also sung Hans' songs, the sad and the beautiful, and especially the one she liked the most: about the sweetheart who lived by the mill and disappeared one day, and the ring that cracked in two. About the boy left behind, who wanted to travel the world as a musician, yet was at a complete loss.

Do I hear the mill wheel turn:
I don't know what I wish –
If I could, I would die,
Then it would desist!

Minna had loved this verse, and often used to sing it to herself.

He had thought he could hear a humming, wings beating, a whimper drifting up from the valley, across the treetops, into this frosty stillness which became entangled in his clothes, penetrating his skin; freezing what was inside him, as though even his heart were turning to ice.

His life had been frozen in time that day, something he had feared even back then: whatever was still to come, it would be an After, a life with the image of his family standing there, as though welded together, and above the image the words, running like a never-ending reel: ... *it's better this way, Sebastian will take on the farm.*

A shiver of cold had driven him onwards, uphill, into the snow, into the wind; he fled as though he were being pursued by dark hordes, nocturnal figures and demons, led by Perchta, hunting him over the peaks of the Grafenberg, the Schnaitberg and down the ravine into the Nordrach valley, to the bridge, to the Jewish cemetery, where he fell to his knees and sank into the snow.

He walked slowly now, on this late afternoon decades later, still on the move in the hope of finding answers to so many questions. Knowing that his brother was on the farm: grown tired, embittered perhaps, an irascible old man who looked out only on the dead, their father, their mother, Minna – a dark host that moved up the valley during the Twelve Nights.

*

He had paused by the crucifix back then too. By the old paddocks, their wood faded like the boards of the shed and stables, and he stood before them, bewildered, uncomprehending, disbelieving: the farm was going to his brother, not him. He had wanted to stay there, on that spot by the stream between the hill and the hunter's lookout, with a view of the black pines and the scattering of birches; he had wanted to live there with Minna. What would she say when she came, after New Year's? Or did she already know? Was she initiated into the plan, part of the conspiracy?

His brother, who had said he wanted to become a hat maker, who had even begun an apprenticeship with the straw-hat makers in Zell, the brother who preferred singing in the choir to working in the fields, amid the grinding of plough and harrow, who knew nothing about tilling and felling, about slaughters and orchards. His brother would be the one on the farm, not him, the farm which he had been promised, as the elder son, he who had learned the ropes and was ready; the farmer, the rightful heir?

It was in this paddock that his plan for revenge had taken shape: the horse would be his retribution for the betrayal.

For a moment, the image of the other man who had been struck by misfortune resurfaced, the man who had lost the woman he loved to the rich farmer. He could picture Lene and Hans so vividly before him.

Lene had stood before the wayside cross beneath the Vogt's house many times, gazing up at it pleadingly as the setting sun cast its light across hill and valley, as the silence expanded down to the stream below. A note of Lene's pain had reverberated in Minna's voice as she told the story, especially when she stressed that no song had been capable of changing the father's mind. Lene had also sung into the silence around her, as though it were possible to sway all the spirits, all the gods.

In this world there's no greater pain,
than to be forbidden from loving,
the heart you long to claim.

He knew the verse from Minna's narrative, and heard her voice. Only later had he read his own pain in it, along with the suffering of everyone who had loved and lost. In this, all lovers were equal, throughout history.

Lene had gone in vain with a sachet of herbs in hand to the chapel, where the Guardian of the Capuchin monks had reminded her that hardship is part of life, that it strikes all who live in this vale of tears, but that it was to be tolerated, without complaint, so she might one day welcome happiness.

Lene had fallen ill. Just three months after her wedding to the rich farmer, a two-horse carriage pulled her coffin down to the cemetery in Zell.

What had cost Minna her sanity, and her life?

He brushed the snow from the bench and touched the crucifix lightly.

It seemed to him that a story told, a story from the past, would never truly fade once it had moved someone. The act of remembering, of reading, was like a return, a homecoming into a story. He was never closer to himself than in the remembered and read.

IV

He stood in the dark for a while, shivering with cold. No light emerged from the house; snow covered the forecourt and the steps leading up to the front door. Icicles jutted from the eaves, stabbing towards the ground. No wheel tracks led down the Hullert road, which disappeared between the trees, the white-cloaked alders and low-hanging willows.

No sound, no movement. Nothing but a thin trail of smoke, rising from the chimney.

He saw the letter box, the metal lined with a seam of white snow. The doorbell on the wall at chest height, beneath it a sign.

His thumb twitched inside his glove.

No.

The word passed soundlessly over his lips.

Why had he been unable to imagine that this farm could one day be his brother's; his hearth and home? Because Sebastian had never seemed suited to be a farmer, a property owner; he was meek, teased at school, mocked or avoided by the girls, someone who remained at the edge of the dance floor, always without a partner, barely noticed, someone who had hardly any friends, who came home with bad grades, who often seemed remorseful, clumsy, at school functions too, eventually slipping away out into the night, preferring to spend his time with the horses, talking to them as though they were the only beings he trusted. That was where Manfred had found him late one evening, as their school days neared an end and the time came for his brother to set his sights on an apprenticeship, to make a decision. He who wanted nothing but to be with the animals.

Turning around, he spotted the tree stump on the forecourt and shivered. That was where it had lain. His worst act – his final act – in their fraternal feud: one too many. Everything before that had been harmless; the slashed car tyres, the unlocked stable door; even their fight, close to the paddling spot in the river. They had laid into each other ferociously: two young men driven by rage, trapped by hopelessness; incapable of conversing, of understanding. Jacob and Esau, or already Cain and Abel?

In the valley, everyone had talked about the war between the brothers. No one intervened, not even their parents. Only the pastor attempted to speak with them, but in vain.

And then the idea had come to him: the horse. Sebastian loved one of them over all the rest, and called it affectionately by name: *Amaro*. He would ride it for hours on end, over the Taschenkopf and down along the Harmersbach stream, whose banks were silted up and shaded by trees. Horses were perhaps the only thing Sebastian truly loved. That was where he wanted to strike him, wound him, teach him a lesson. So great was his indignation, so painful his humiliation that his brother had outmanoeuvred him. His brother, who as it turned out wasn't clumsy at all, but instead had surreptitiously found ways to win over their mother. Through flattery, false promises, lies? Then their father. Eventually, it would be Minna too: she was all he had left. She too a figure in the deceitful plan.

He had screamed his rage up to the heavens, and couldn't be calmed by anything, not even the pastor's conciliatory tone or the verger's rational words. He wanted to hurt Sebastian just as he himself had been hurt. He wanted to get back at him, to avenge himself. To be hard, unrelenting. Nothing he had inflicted on Sebastian had been enough. Until the horse.

Later, much later, he felt ashamed. But by then it was too late, and the shame lived on; the memory always returned at Christmastime. He even heard the humming in his foreign home, where no one spoke of ghostly processions, of kobolds and wights; he would hear the animal's whimpers and groans, his brother's cries.

How could he have done something like that, back then in the week between the years? And to curse his brother, too.

Hadn't he realised there would be no more discussion after that, not even with his parents? No one had understood. Not even

Minna. They were united by their disgust, by their rejection of someone who was capable of such a thing. Minna loved horses too. Was that why she sided with Sebastian?

Once, the three of them had gone riding together, up the Langenberg to the lookout point over the Vosges mountain range; Seb in front, Minna behind him, Manfred bringing up the rear. They were planning to climb the tower, to gaze across the Rhine valley and into Alsace, to the places they longed for, to Strasbourg, where the other world was; life itself.

But Sebastian fell from his horse and cut his head open. Minna had tended to him, dabbing away the blood as she cradled his head in her lap. Had that been the start of it all? Should he have suspected what would come later?

Snow lay deep in the forecourt; white and empty. He pictured the animal, snorting with agony, writhing around, its body in spasm.

Would he be able to speak with his brother now?

He had heard about all the misfortune which had befallen him, out in the fields, among his livestock. With Minna – that most of all. Sebastian had never answered Manfred's letters. But he wasn't the type for letter writing. Even talking was difficult for him. Stubborn, they had called him at school, mulish.

And now?

The white envelope shook in his hand. There was just one word written on it: Sebastian.

His brother had always loved his name, as well as its abbreviation, Seb, which he sometimes tacked on, with a soft *e*, drawn out, and a pause after the *b* that seemed like an abyss, an open mouth.

Would he even find the letter, would he read it? A few words about the New Year, together with the request – concise, urgent – that he come and meet him.

No attempt at persuasion, for his brother wouldn't like that, nor any word about his illness. A guilty conscience clung to both of them; the propensity to justify themselves, even for the mere fact of being there.

In the letter, he was asking his brother to come and speak with him one more time. He shuffled across the forecourt, climbed the two steps, lifted the metal lid, pushed the letter through the gap.

The sign no longer bore a name; the paper was saturated, warped. His thumb moved once more towards the doorbell, trembling.

No.

He turned away abruptly and tramped down to the road. Should he go straight back to the inn?

The fog descended once more, pushing its way down between the dark tree trunks. Yet he clambered resolutely further, up the valley; wheel tracks showed him the way. The wind rippled across the embankment, which sloped down to the stream. A sign pointed towards the nearby farmsteads, another to the Vogt auf Mühlstein. But the path was nowhere to be seen. On the hillside above, a house crouched beneath the snow, no light in its windows.

The wind strengthened, gusts that swept the flakes of snow into his face, more forcefully than even minutes before. His gaze followed the wheel tracks, which were still just about visible, as were the trees amidst the grey, the stream down below. His breathing was laboured. He paused, shocked by how swiftly the darkness was intensifying, as though ink-black clouds were on the move, disguising his surroundings, swallowing everything which just moments ago had still possessed shape and form. The snow had become a flickering, fast and impetuous, as though the wind – or perhaps it was already a storm – were in control now, steering the snowflakes, the night, his footsteps.

Would he soon freeze over with sleet, and fossilise into a monument to the curse and fraternal feud, from which a moaning and rattling would be heard, in the dark forests and bleak moors, in the ravines and on the icy slopes, a creaking perhaps, a wailing?

He stamped his feet, wiped the wetness from his face. He struggled for air, struggled with what was haunting him, the wind roaring and howling from the treetops, from the summits and ledges. He wrapped his arms around his torso, tightly at first, then more slackly, then barely at all –

V

Was he the one flailing his hands, his out-stretched arms clearing a path, making space, wanting to forge ahead through the shivering and shaking?

He heard voices through the wadding that surrounded him, floating up and down; his ears, his ribs, everywhere throbbed and pounded, the kind of pain that burrowed, pinched, hammered, gouged. He searched for words, his own, which would push their way through the cocoon, to the others, to the voices outside.

Sebastian?

The word came slowly, with a pleading undertone, one of hope.

We've sent word. He's sure to come, don't worry.

He slowly opened his eyes, becoming aware of the band of light. Was he the one lying there? Elevated amidst the white of the blankets, sweating and shivering, trying to hold on, not only with his hands, but with words too.

Fever, he heard now, inflammation, the doctor will be back this evening, for now just rest, just wait a little.

He closed his eyes, dug his fingers into the blanket, let himself drift. Sleep a little, wait a little –

He would come, his brother had promised he would join him later, up at the hut where they planned to spend the night, out in unfamiliar hunting grounds, until dawn. He, Manfred, had set off first, making his way slowly uphill through the late summer night. He heard a snapping sound in the undergrowth, then a scraping. He continued on hesitantly, looking all around him, jumping at every noise, telling himself to be brave. They had decided to keep their expedition a secret, to stay out all night: an adventure and a test of courage. They wanted to be runaways, like Tom and Huck. Their stream was no Mississippi river, admittedly, but night-time could be eerie in Hullert too. He heard a hissing and rustling, a deer or wolf, a fox probably, a hare for sure. This was their magical realm, one that could provoke fear when a buzzard's call echoed mournfully out of the ravine, breaking the quietude of the cold slopes; when something unknown drew near.

There was also a cave, towards Höllhaken and the Hagenbach mountains. Other nocturnal treasure hunters had ventured there too, unafraid of the demons.

He heard the wind rushing and whistling down from the mountain, the caw of the ravens from Erbsengrund. The darkness grew, the night. The fear.

His brother would come.

He had waited by the hut, by the bench, hour after hour until daybreak. Sebastian never came. But their father did, and he beat him right there in the forest, ordering him onto the tractor and taking him home. As punishment, rather than painting fences, he had to muck out the stables. He had resented his brother, for leaving him waiting.

*

He had always been waiting for something, in vain. For the farm. For Minna.

The image always preceded her: Minna's bright, laughing face, in defiance of the day, the weather, of everything that tried to be heavy, as though she had surrendered its weight to the heavens. She was there long before she actually arrived, a slender figure, floating into the room with winged lightness, like a dizzily reeling moth, or the ochre-toned, dill-infatuated swallowtail in the August light. She seemed to tumble out of the frayed shadows of a late summer afternoon, when the sunbeams flowed through the trees in white stria. A fragrance suffused the room: the image of her flickered within it, as though she wanted to play their lovers' games in flight.

And then, when she appeared in the doorway and raised her hand in greeting, he moved towards her through the transfiguration, amazed that she wasn't a phantom but a person, wearing shoes and a bag thrown over her shoulder, uttering a greeting which sounded mortal, and typically abrupt for the local Baden dialect: *Guete Dag.*

Minna never came again.

No one had come to walk by his side, not even in the distant land.

After Minna, the paths remained empty and untrodden; the longing for arrival unfulfilled.

You're the kind of person who spends their whole life waiting, he had sometimes thought to himself.

Another bout of shivering, first hot, then cold, an icy chill that shot through him. His eyelids burned; his cheeks blazed. He wrapped his arms around his chest as though he were still out in the driving snow, in the shimmering and flickering which had taken possession of him, awakening a trepidation, a dark foreboding.

The doctor will be here soon, your brother too.

He heard the voice once more. It reached him through the pain, the knocking and pounding.

Try to rest, just wait a little longer.

*

Like he had waited back then, on the final day before his departure, in the hope that, despite everything, everything unspeakable, appalling, abominable – whichever word he wanted to use – Minna would come and talk with him one more time.

His love for her filled the waiting, expanding in the room and drifting out into the landscape.

He had asked her, politely, urgently, and also by letter, to come and meet him, suggesting the small tavern not far from Michaelskapelle, where the road climbed towards Kirnbach. They could have spoken undisturbed there, or even walked out into the countryside a little, so he could give her a last heartfelt word and perhaps hear a conciliatory one in return; something to ease his journey, the memory, the goodbye.

Or had he hoped she would stop him from leaving, ask him to stay and attempt a conversation with his brother, maybe even a reconciliation?

Was he making up for it now, decades later, as though what had been lost could be regained, and grievances healed?

Should he have stayed back then? If he had, would his life have taken a different course? Perhaps one that included Minna, after all, sharing in one of the plans they had made?

He had once travelled to the Vosges with Minna, late one summer. They hiked from the village of Fouday along a narrow path through the mountains, high above the Steintal valley, the stream far below even more lively than the one back home, curving through the meadows and eroding the river-bank. The alders cast their shadow pattern on the grass, which was still a vibrant green, even in the refracted light. The path became damp and marshy as they neared Waldersbach, the puddles reflecting proces-sions of clouds that drifted like feathers through the blue. They held hands as Minna pointed out holy rope and impatiens, and a yellowhammer which sat on a fence, guarding the valley. At the edge of the forest, where the village and parsonage came into view, they saw the black-as-night shimmer of the elderberry bushes which clung to the farmsteads along the road. Minna was fond of the simple stone houses, especially their door- and window-frames, carefully hewn from red sandstone. There was a trickling fountain every few metres, the kind an aspiring pastor could have stumbled into at night, to drive out the visions, his pain over the young woman, Friederike, who wouldn't be his or anyone else's, not since the master. But only by Oberlin's parsonage was the basin of the fountain shallow enough for bathing. That was where Minna had said for the first time that she wanted to stay in the village.

Yet she didn't want to see the parsonage. The vibrancy of the summer colours, the brightness of the day, drew them uphill, to where newlyweds had planted an *allée* of linden trees; the embankment covered with tansy, Vosges roses, fringed orchids. Minna had stood there in reverent silence, as though they were making their way upwards through the gates of heaven, just as, long ago, someone had walked through the mountains in search of arrival.

Towards the mountain hostel at the end of the *allée*, a green expanse opened up, sparsely scattered with heather and wild flowers. Pastor Oberlin had often ridden out here to visit the lonely dwellings; the solitary figures in their ramshackle farmhouses, receiving no visitors but him.

This could be our valley too, said Minna suddenly, handing him a sprig of heather. We could learn a trade, breed horses, the two of us back home in Reichstal, or elsewhere.

Oberlin had cultivated flax and cotton, despite the harsh climate in the Vosges, in order to provide work for the women, to boost the spinning trade and establish weaving mills; he was a man who was always on the move, initially with his wife, and later with the curate, Louise.

They too could start something like that, he and Minna. They had already forged plans for a life on the farm, had deliberated between flax, legumes, new varieties of potato.

There was to be a place for Sebastian in their plans too, if he wanted it, caring for the animals he loved, tending to the woods that were so dear to him.

At the end of that day, they went to the Fouday cemetery: *Père Oberlin*, it said on his grave, a wooden cross, nothing more. Somewhere close by, Minna commented, must be the grave of the child whom Lenz had tried in vain to heal and then to bring back to life, because she had the same name as his great love: Friederike.

Sebastian hadn't wanted to accompany them on their journey through the valley; even Minna's urging was futile. They waited a long while, but he never came.

It was impossible to see a thing outside the window now, only white, a glimmer in his fevered delirium, a howling storm.

The snow was relentless back then too, on that January day at the inn near Michaelskapelle; he had lingered and stalled, sitting by the window with his gaze fixed on the road, so he would see at once if a vehicle approached, or if a figure, dainty and delicate, came up the hill with small strides. Minna could perhaps come with the horse-drawn sleigh, maybe accompanied by her brother, or even her mother, white shapes that would emerge from yet more white, carrying before them white images, white sheets, unwritten.

No one had come along the road, not even from Kirnbach, Anhalden or Lehgrund. The snow held everyone inside their homes, in repose after the New Year festivities, letting their pounding skulls unpickle and overstuffed bellies dry out. The colourful Christmas lights still hung in the café, and scattered here and there were the shards of a shattered bauble or a few threads of silvery tinsel, a burned-out sparkler.

The landlord was nowhere to be seen, and his daughters stared sullenly into the distance, their exaggerated yawns making it all too clear that they would rather have stayed in bed than do this New Year's shift. The snow continued to fall. He would have to leave early for the train station the next day in order to reach

Frankfurt in time, for there were sure to be delays.

From where did he find the hope that she might still come; talk to him; find a way to forgive?

On that New Year's Sunday, all the plans he'd made with Minna had passed through his mind once more, some of them illuminated momentarily by a flicker of hope.

He had waited on into the evening, giving it another half-hour, then yet another. Even long after the landlord's daughters' yawning had become ill-humoured throat clearing, and eventually disgruntled coughing, he had drunk another coffee, another water, another spritzer, and had read, after the *Badische Zeitung*, then the *Schwarzwälder Post* and the parish newsletter, followed, multiple times, by the menu.

Minna hadn't come.

He had spent a restless night in Zell, then left without a word, without a goodbye. And something had remained unresolved, returning to haunt him even in the foreign land, holding its ground, unsettling him over and over, not fading either with time or with life.

He had never spoken with Minna again.

Later, much later, she wrote him a few words: a letter, which reached him after a circuitous route.

That someone like you, she wrote, a few months after his departure, *that a person whom I loved could do such a thing, driven by a vengefulness so alien to me, so cold, thinking only of blind revenge, lashing out wildly, even sending an animal to an agonising death – that pushed me away, severed a bond that was tightly woven, for me too. You know how much I loved you. Your disappointment over the lost inheritance was understandable; your vindictiveness was not. It was a rift that no conversation could heal. And later, much later, not rashly or blindly, it led me to turn towards the man who was also fond of me, who also loved me. Not because he was now the heir, but because he was the gentler of you both, and perhaps the more helpless and vulnerable.*

Different to you, but lovable in his own way;
needy, one could say.

He had read the letter many times, falling
with its words back into the tenderness he felt
for Minna. It lived on through all the years.
'For ever. And all eternity.' It awoke in every
present, even now, in these bleak nights at the
end of the century.

He hadn't attended Minna's burial. He
hadn't been able to bring himself to stand
before the grave with the others who were sure
to flock to the cemetery. He had feared the
hostile looks, the whispers reminding people
of the old story. To stand there amongst them,
by all the graves behind the pilgrimage church,
was something he wouldn't have been able to
bear. Something had broken open deep inside
him, a rupture, painful to the touch. And
Sebastian? How could he have faced him again,
after all those years, and by Minna's grave, of all
places? Would they have come to blows even
there?

Hans, in his day, had gone to Lene's
burial, receiving thirteen hours' leave from

the Imperial Rhine Army during the Siege of Haguenau. He hurried across the Rhine to the grave behind the church, laid wild chrysanthemums below the cross, then looked up at the valley, a stranger returned home, and groaned beneath the weight of a great love that never faded, not even after death. He fell in the battle.

This time it wasn't the voices or the pain in his eyes and ears, nor the hot and cold, the frenzy of images and fevered dreams, but the sound of the evening church bells coming from afar, reaching him like the edge of a wave retreating gently from the shore.

In its wake came a waft of incense, of poppy seed and herbal balms.

He heard the stairs creaking, the monotonous sing-song of the pastor and altar boys.

With shuffling steps, the ageing pastor made his way across the room, said a blessing at the bedside, and exhorted the expulsion of all remaining evil from the year gone by, the old year's spirits. Everything unresolved, he said, touching Manfred's shoulder, all that which has not yet passed, that too shall release its hold.

Manfred nodded his head gently, breathing in the scent that hung in the room, drawing it through his nose with a light sniffle, as though it were redemption and relief. And he saw before him his mother, who on New Year's Eve and Epiphany had gone through the house with her solstice bundles of hazel, oak leaves and mountain arnica. She seemed strangely close now. The scent had lingered in the house for days on end; heavy, penetrating. No one besides their mother had believed in its effect, but they would have missed it if it wasn't there. Sebastian used to hum as she worked.

If he were to describe his childhood, these scents would be it. They were there long before the words, and evoked the images that never fade, the embraces that linger on; an arrival, perhaps, or more, childhoodland, the scents of the Twelve Nights, Epiphany.

He slept from the old year into the new, only hearing now and then, in brief moments of awakening and stirring, the noise downstairs in the bar, the battle of words between Lutz, the verger and the landlord, the brandy-loosened tongues, the exuberance and dance of clinking glasses.

In his sporadic moments of wakefulness, his attention went to the voices. Who was there, who was speaking? Voices amid the clatter of crockery, the slurping and smacking. The food must be heavy, tough; the chewing was vigorous. Roast pork, perhaps, or even wild boar, its sturdy bones defying every knife and making an adventure of the hunt for a scrap of meat.

For New Year's Eve, their mother had always prepared a platter of boiled pork belly and sausages, with sauerkraut from the earthenware pot in the cellar. The well-seasoned Leberwurst were her speciality; Sebastian had been particularly fond of them.

He heard a creaking in the stairwell, a toilet being flushed, Lutz's loud and dominant voice, the verger, who seemed to be correcting him, or perhaps merely placating, when Lutz evoked the demons and reminded them of the water spirits in Mummelsee; the earth spirits deep in the forests and ravines of the Harmersbach valley; the madwomen roaming through the gloomy marshlands and fog-saturated heathlands.

There was another voice, too, joining in more hesitantly, telling of snow at the foothills of the valley, of toppled trees, of impending doom across the land.

Someone interrupted with *Prost!* Glasses thudded together.

Then the hesitant voice again, barely audible.

Who did it belong to? Sebastian?

And Lutz once more, interjecting loudly, scraps of his sentences reaching Manfred's sickbed, pushing their way to his ears – about these dark times, the cracks, the uncertainties.

Then someone else began to hold forth, as though everything had to be said hurriedly while it was still the old year, or prophesied for the coming one. Abundance and stillness. Celestial blessings, the future as a vulnerable word.

*

That wasn't Sebastian's voice.

He fell back into a deep sleep.

Slept on and heard nothing.

Not even the clamour at midnight reached him, the din of popping corks, the fireworks over the rolling hills which spluttered stars and drew threadsuns in the night sky.

The doctor had come, bringing medicine that made him doze. The landlord had wished him a happy New Year; Bettine had put flowers and some New Year's cake on the table. He didn't want to eat, and drank tea only reluctantly.

From time to time he opened his eyes and looked out of the window, into the snowy landscape, at the dark trees, hearing the croak of the ravens, the bang of a rocket fired belatedly into the New Year's sky.

He let himself be carried by long-gone images and scents: Minna was there; his brother; his mother, burning her herbs. He saw within the white blur a figure coming uphill, wearing a hat pulled down low, hunched over, slow like someone who was in no hurry to arrive, who has time and needs time, to be there, somewhen.

Once, he awoke and saw the snow on the windowsill, bunched like frills of mousseline; behind it, the shimmer and flicker of the snow-covered landscape. A shiver ran across his skin and ebbed away.

Again he closed his eyes.

They were coming towards him: Minna, his brother, his mother, slowly through the snow. He listened to hear what they were saying, or perhaps calling out. Names?

He hoped it was his.

When he opened his eyes again, everything was silent; outside the window there was nothing but white, erasing all form. Nothing to see, nothing to hold on to, just a flood of white, without words, without sound. White that expanded through the windows and doors, into his eyes and mouth, into his skin, his breath; the snow, overrunning, overgrowing, engulfing.

*

And then a commotion, a rattling, a wailing; the clatter of pots. Shouting, incomprehensible but loud, murmuring, mumbling.

The creak of the door, a draught of air, the landlord's heavy footsteps crossing the room to his bed.

They're on the move, Holda and Perchta, with their hordes, shaking out their sacks, coming down from Nordrach, from the Grafenberg and the Taschenkopf, screaming and dancing. An unholy din, as you know, when Epiphany draws near and the Twelve Nights are at an end, when the evil spirits retreat and everything that was out of joint, the time and the world, falls into place.

Into place? he asked in a weak voice.

He heard the landlord wheeze, saw behind his closed eyes the wild horde of Perchtas, swinging their whips, drumming, and amongst them a high sound, a lute, a flute. And a melody that he knew from his mother. Songs of the Twelve Nights, she had said, as she hummed and burned her herbs.

Their mother always joined the procession, in a white mask that hid her face, and a white robe. Minna accompanied her. Along with the other women from the farms, they made their way along the stream to the valley, to the bonfire, gathering around it, throwing into the flames mementoes of hardships suffered, of everything that had gone by. The special cakes made the previous day flew into the fire too, the biscuits and groats which were loved by the invisible ghosts.

He heard the stairs creak again, more audibly with every hesitant step, fraying out into a dull thud along the corridor, a timid echo, close by. A heavy shoe stepped into the room, moving forwards and dragging the other behind it, shuffling over to his bedside.

Someone, said the landlord, close to his ear, someone has come up through the grey, through the snow, and is here to see you.

Slowly he opened his eyes, blinked once, twice, lifted his hand gently.

Sebastian.

Manfred.

THE LEOPARD

The leopard is one of Harvill's historic colophons and an imprimatur of the highest quality literature from around the world.

When The Harvill Press was founded in 1946 by former Foreign Office colleagues Manya Harari and Marjorie Villiers (hence Har-vill), it was with the express intention of rebuilding cultural bridges after the Second World War. As their first catalogue set out: 'The editors believe that by producing translations of important books they are helping to overcome the barriers, which at present are still big, to close interchange of ideas between people who are divided by frontiers.' The press went on to publish from many different languages, with highlights including Giuseppe Tomasi di Lampedusa's *The Leopard*, Boris Pasternak's *Doctor Zhivago*, José Saramago's *Blindness*, W. G. Sebald's *The Rings of Saturn*,

Henning Mankell's *Faceless Killers* and Haruki Murakami's *Norwegian Wood*.

In 2005 The Harvill Press joined with Secker & Warburg, a publisher with its own illustrious history of publishing international writers. In 2020, Harvill Secker reintroduced the leopard to launch a new translated series celebrating some of the finest and most exciting voices of the twenty-first century.

Laurent Binet: *Civilisations*
    trans. Sam Taylor
Paolo Cognetti: *Without Ever Reaching the Summit*
    trans. Stash Luczkiw
Pauline Delabroy-Allard: *All About Sarah*
    trans. Adriana Hunter
Urs Faes: *Twelve Nights*
    trans. Jamie Lee Searle
Ismail Kadare: *The Doll*
    trans. John Hodgson
Jonas Hassen Khemiri: *The Family Clause*
    trans. Alice Menzies

Karl Ove Knausgaard: *In the Land of the Cyclops: Essays*
   trans. Martin Aitken
Karl Ove Knausgaard: *The Morning Star*
   trans. Martin Aitken
Geert Mak: *The Dream of Europe*
   trans. Liz Waters
Ngũgĩ wa Thiong'o: *The Perfect Nine: The Epic of Gikuyu and Mumbi*
   trans. the author
Intan Paramaditha: *The Wandering*
   trans. Stephen J. Epstein
Per Petterson: *Men in My Situation*
   trans. Ingvild Burkey
Dima Wannous: *The Frightened Ones*
   trans. Elisabeth Jaquette